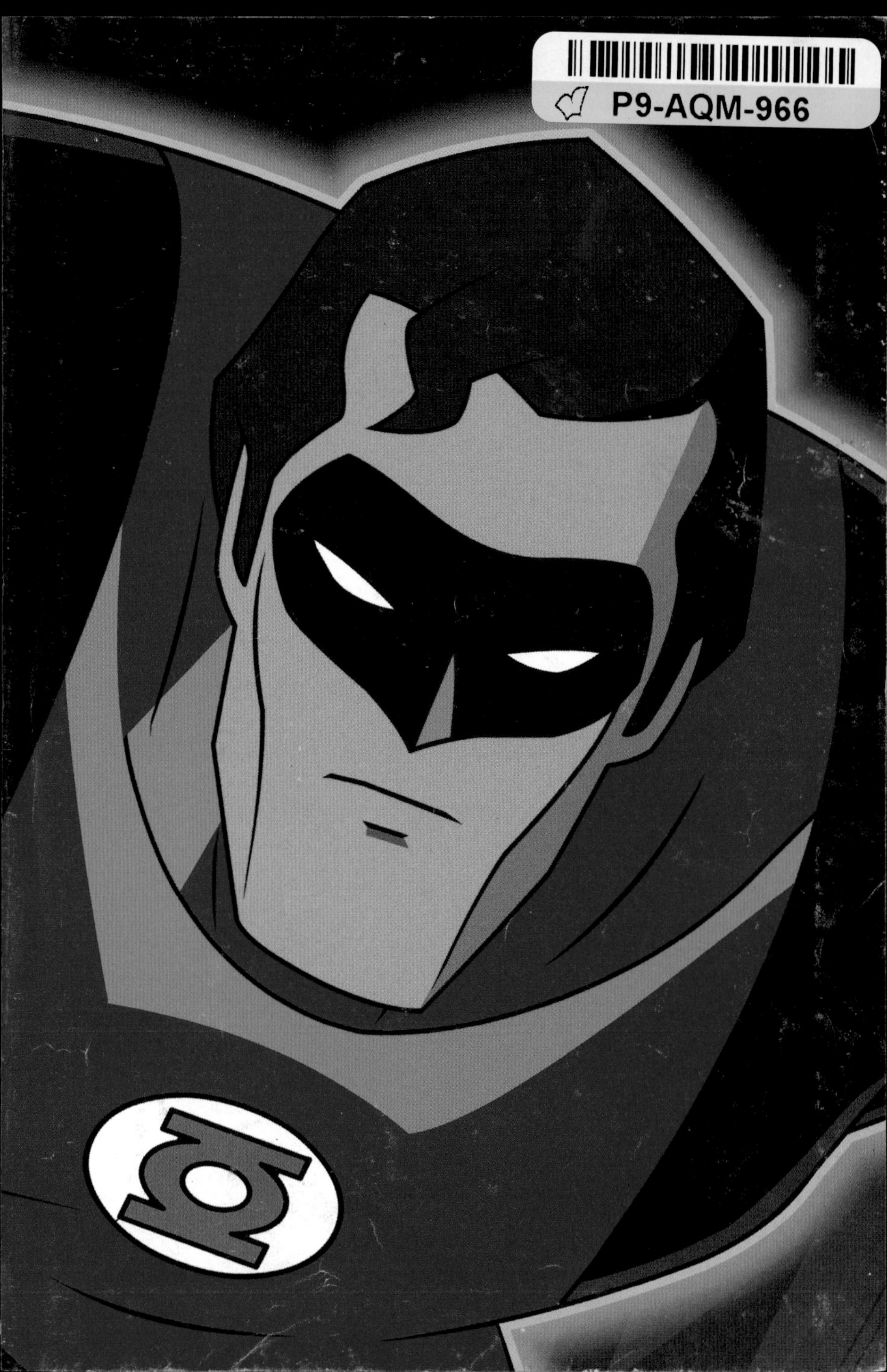

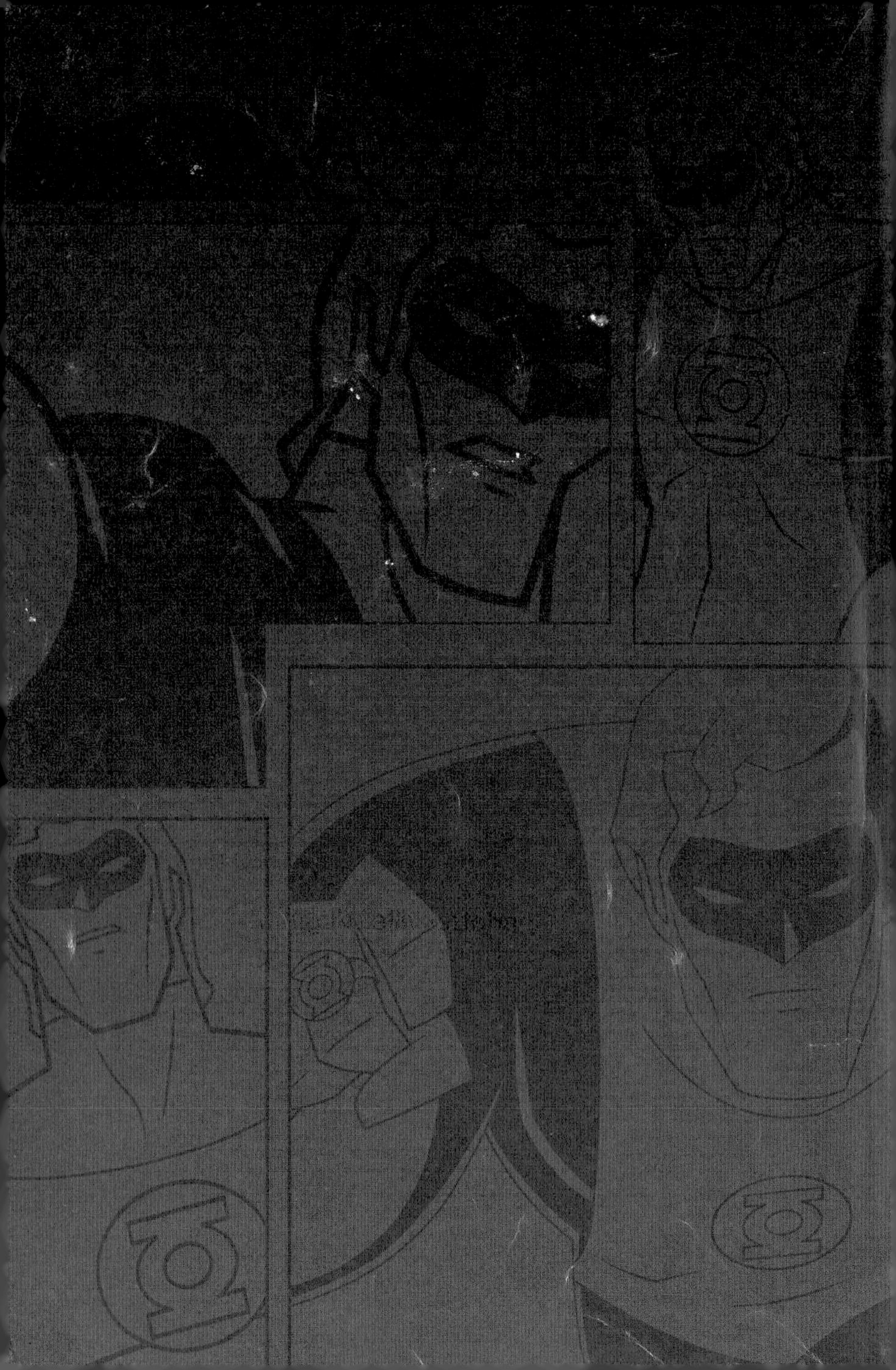

AS THE NEWEST MEMBER OF AN INTERGALACTIC PEACEKEEPING FORCE KNOWN AS THE GREEN LANTERN CORPS, HAL JORDAN FIGHTS EVIL AND PROUDLY WEARS THE UNIFORM AND RING OF . . .

SUPER DC HEROES™

GREEN LANTERN™

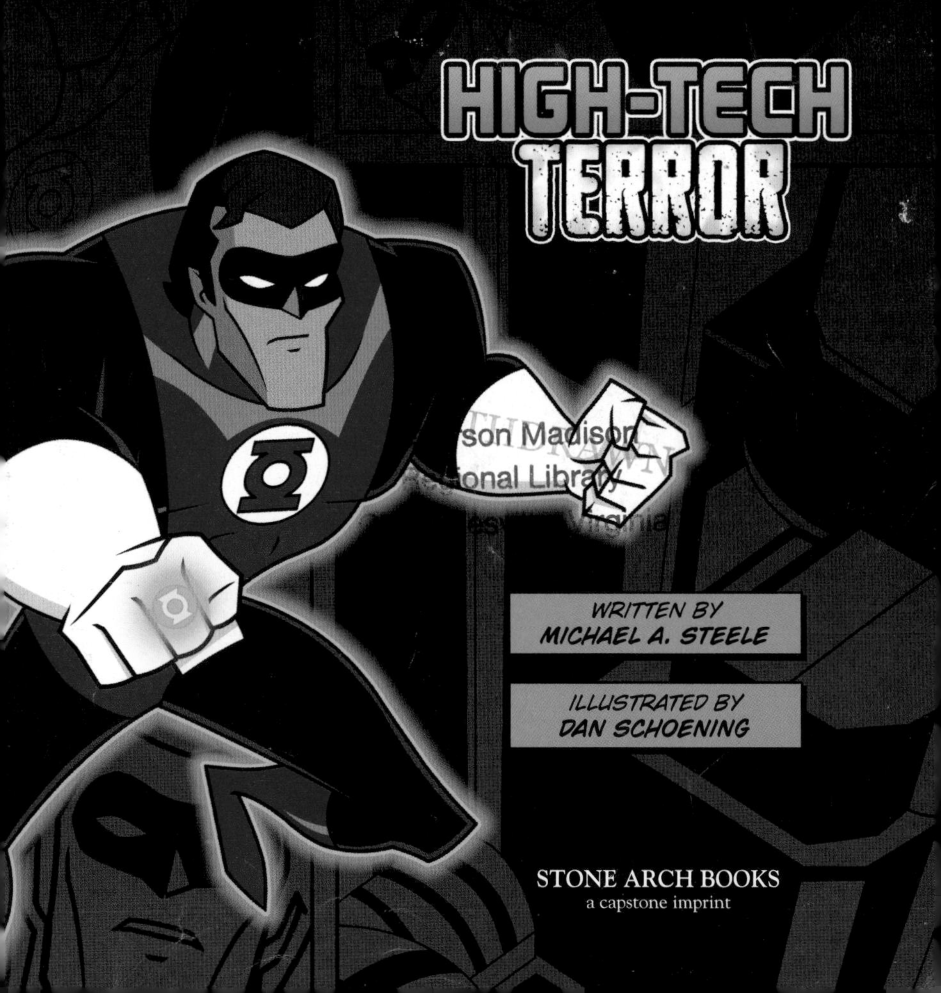

HIGH-TECH TERROR

WRITTEN BY
MICHAEL A. STEELE

ILLUSTRATED BY
DAN SCHOENING

STONE ARCH BOOKS
a capstone imprint

Published by Stone Arch Books in 2011
A Capstone Imprint
151 Good Counsel Drive, P.O. Box 669
Mankato, Minnesota 56002
www.capstonepub.com

Library of Congress Cataloging-in-Publication Data

Steele, Michael Anthony.
   High-tech terror / written by Michael A. Steele ; illustrated by Dan
Schoening.
       p. cm. -- (DC super heroes. Green lantern)
   ISBN 978-1-4342-2609-9 (library binding) -- ISBN 978-1-4342-3084-3 (pbk.)
   1. Graphic novels. [1. Graphic novels. 2. Superheroes--Fiction. 3.
Robots--Fiction.] I. Schoening, Dan, ill. II. Title.
   PZ7.7.S73Hig 2011
   741.5'973--dc22   2010032408

Summary: While on intergalactic patrol, Hal Jordan, a member of the Green
Lantern Corps, receives a distress call. A nearby planet is under attack . . . by
lawn mowers! All of the planet's machines have come alive. Cars, trucks, even
television sets, have transformed into deadly robots. Soon, Hal learns that a
superpowered robot is behind the mechanical chaos. Unfortunately, pulling the
plug on this super-villain won't be easy.

Art Director: Bob Lentz
Designer: Hilary Wacholz
Production Specialist: Michelle Biedscheid

Printed in the United States of America in Stevens Point, Wisconsin.
092010
005934WZS11

TABLE OF CONTENTS

30642 8762
C

CHAPTER 1

TO THE RESCUE! 4

CHAPTER 2

HARDWARE GONE HAYWIRE 14

CHAPTER 3

THE TERROR OF TEKIK 22

CHAPTER 4

ROBOT RAMPAGE 31

CHAPTER 5

THE HEART OF THE PROBLEM 41

TO THE RESCUE!

Hal Jordan zipped past clouds as he soared through the sky. They completely engulfed him as he flew lower. Then the feathery curtain parted, and the ground came into view. The desert landscape grew closer by the second. Just as Hal was near enough to count the needles on a cactus, he pulled up.

ZWWWOOOOMMMM!

With a gloved hand, he pulled back on the plane's control stick. The jet fighter was less than twenty feet from the ground.

A plume of sand followed the jet as it roared toward the airbase. Hal smiled behind the tinted shield of his helmet.

As a test pilot, Hal enjoyed flying the newest and fastest jets the Air Force had to offer. He happily pushed them to their limits. Sometimes, he pushed them past their limits, having to bail out before they crashed. That never bothered him, though. Hal Jordan had no fear.

Hal landed the jet and pulled toward the hangar. He immediately spotted Thomas Kalmaku. The young mechanic was there to greet Hal as he climbed down from the plane.

"How'd she do?" Tommy asked.

"I got her up to Mach 8 without any problems," Hal said. "Quite a thrill!"

Tommy laughed. "Ha! How can that be a thrill?" he asked. "You can fly anywhere in the galaxy with that power ring of yours."

Tommy was one of the few people who new Hal Jordan was a Green Lantern. The Green Lantern Corps was like a police force for the entire universe. Each member wore a special power ring. Each ring gave its owner amazing abilities.

Hal held up his right hand, and the green ring glowed. "That's true," Hal agreed. "But flying a fighter jet is different. If you do it right, the aircraft feels like it's part of you — as if you're one with the machine."

"If you say so," Tommy chuckled.

BEEP! BEEP! BEEP!

Suddenly, Hal's ring flashed, and a voice sounded from it. "Lantern Jordan," the ring said, "your presence is required on the planet Dalnore. Proceed there immediately."

Hal tossed Tommy his helmet. "Looks like playtime is over, Tommy." He held up a fist and his ring blazed brightly. Its glow spread, washing over his body like water. His flight suit transformed into his Green Lantern uniform.

Hal pointed to the jet. "Take care of her for me, will you?" the super hero said, rising off the ground.

"Sure will, Hal —" started Tommy. "Uh, I mean, Green Lantern Jordan!"

Hal waved goodbye as he soared into the sky.

Within seconds, he broke through Earth's atmosphere and rocketed toward the stars.

WHOOOOSH!

His power ring surrounded his body with a glowing force field. It protected him from the vacuum of space. Hal's power ring also gave him the ability to fly out of the solar system at incredible speed. Like a green comet, he zipped past stars and asteroids, heading toward the planet Dalnore.

Within minutes, his target came into view. Dalnore was an agricultural world, mostly covered in farmland. It had only a few major cities and provided food for many nearby planets. The Dalnorians were peaceful farmers who usually got along with everyone. Hal couldn't understand what the emergency might be. He flew closer to the planet.

Hal's ring guided him toward the source of the distress call. He soared past one of the cities and out over the surrounding countryside. Fields of Dalnorian crops stretched to the horizon. A few small villages were sprinkled among the rows of alien corn and beans.

Suddenly, Hal spotted the emergency. Several giant harvesters were on the loose. Instead of tending to individual fields, the huge machines were moving in a long row across all the fields. Their rotating blades sliced up everything in their paths. They were cutting their way toward a nearby village. Frightened Dalnorians fled from their homes, screaming with terror!

As Hal flew closer, he noticed a Dalnorian driving one of the harvesters.

"Is that the guy who's controlling these machines?" Hal asked. "If so, this is going to be easy."

Hal hovered and aimed his ring at the large farming machine. A beam of green energy burst from the ring. The energy formed into a giant hand that plucked the driver from the harvester. Hal made the hand dangle the driver in front of him.

"What are you doing?" Hal asked the man. "Why are you trying to destroy this village?"

"I wasn't," explained the driver. "I was trying to stop them! We don't know what's wrong with the harvesters."

As Hal moved the driver to safety, another beam burst from his ring.

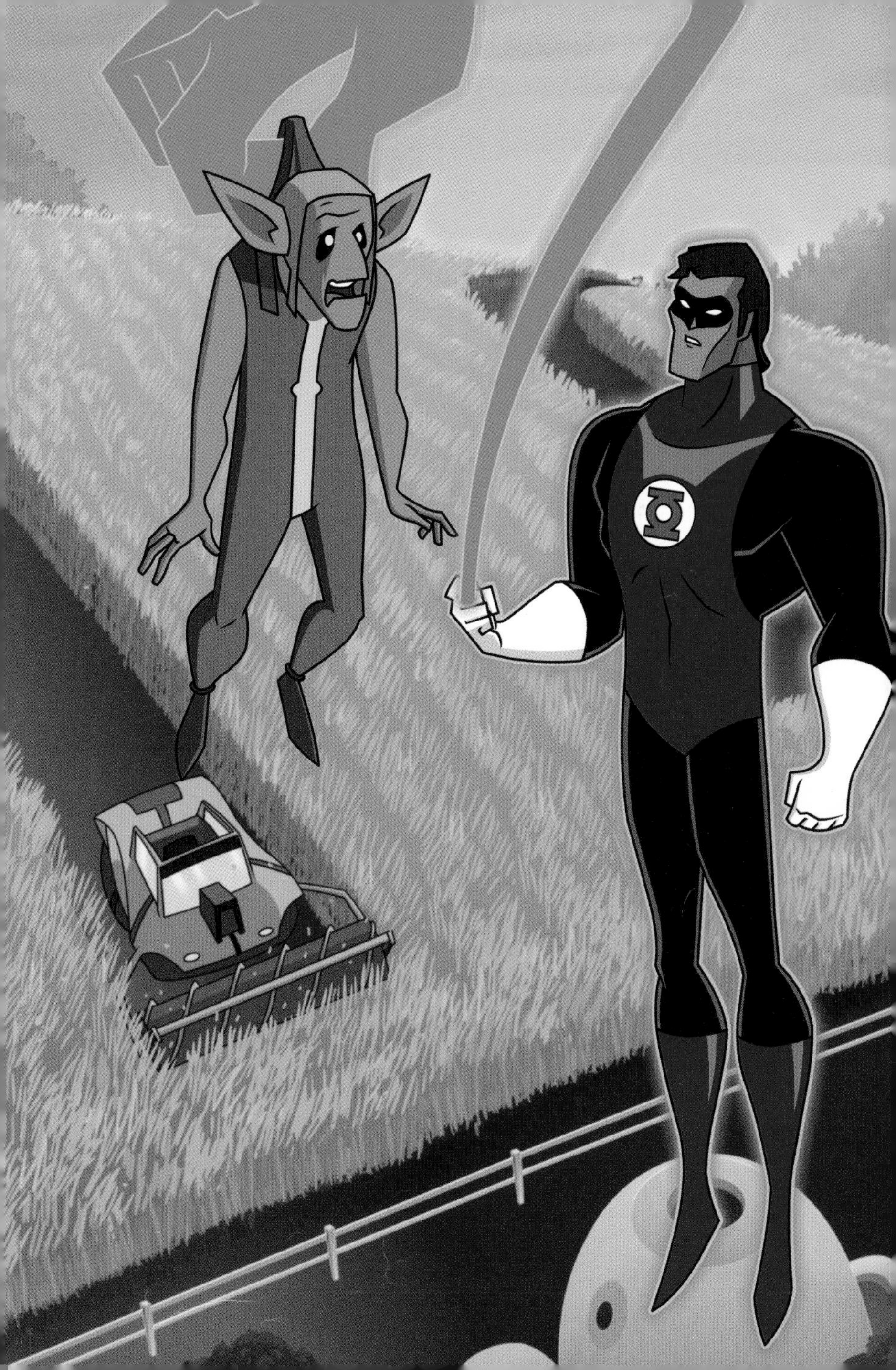

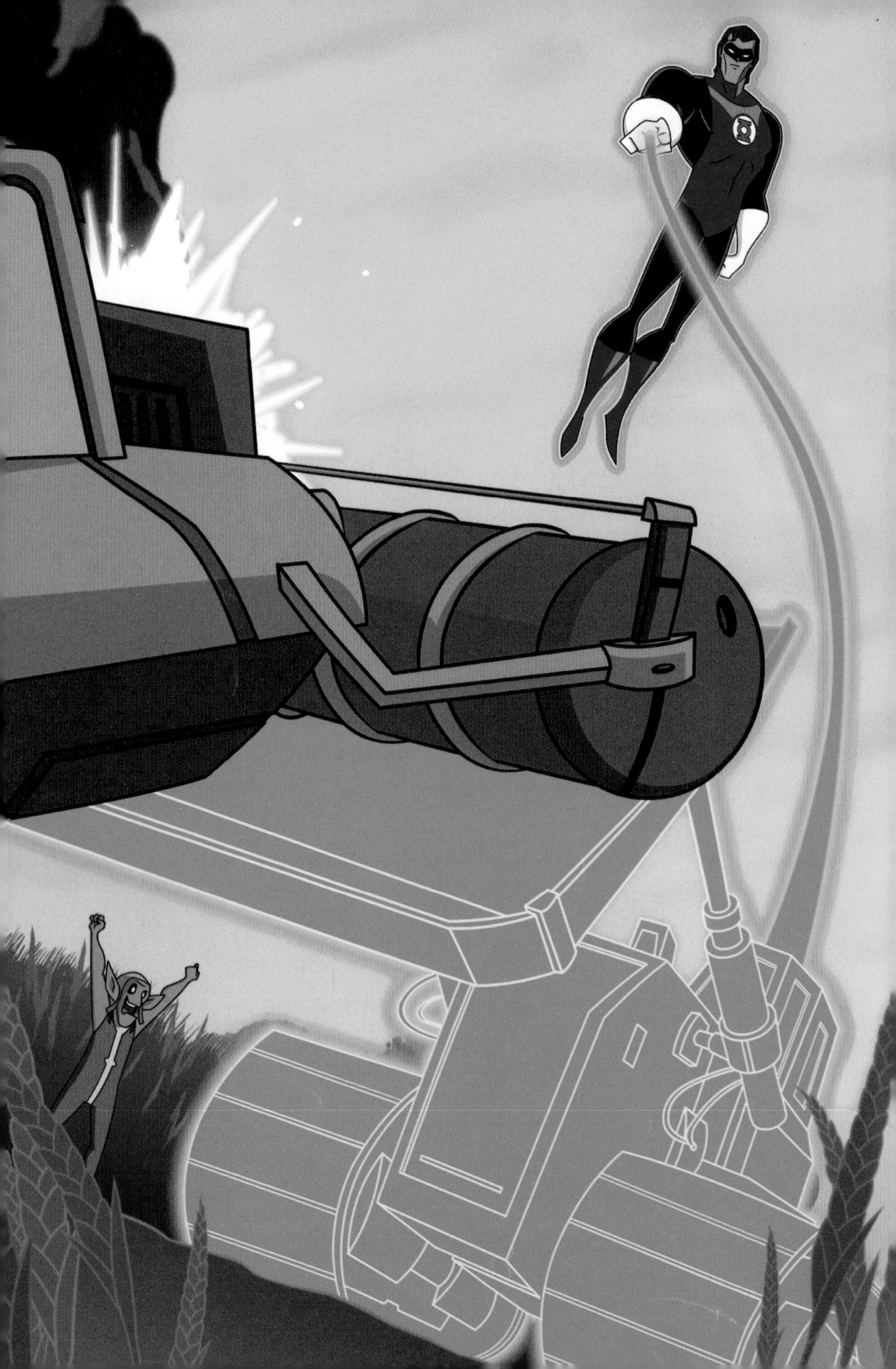

The green beam formed into several big green bulldozers. The trucks smashed into the harvesters, pushing them away from the village. The harvesters continued chugging forward until their engines smoked. One by one, they shut down. Soon, they were a line of lifeless, smoking hulks.

The Dalnorians cheered. Hal was about to inspect one of the harvesters when his ring sounded again. "Emergency in the nearby city!" announced the ring.

"What now?" asked Hal, heading toward the alert. As he flew closer, he heard screams.

CHAPTER 2

HARDWARE GONE HAYWIRE

Hal flew into the alien city, which appeared similar to the ones on Earth. Tall, window-covered skyscrapers reached to the sky. Crisscrossing streets and sidewalks separated the buildings. Citizens crowded the sidewalks.

However, this city didn't have cars and buses like Hal's home planet. The Dalnorians traveled in hover cars. But something was wrong. The flying machines had gone crazy! Drivers fought with the controls of their hover cars.

The floating vehicles smashed into each other. Glass sprayed from the buildings as the cars scraped their sides. Cement flew into the air as they crashed into sidewalks.

WHAM! Dalnorians dived for cover as the hover cars zigzagged around them.

Hal flew over the city streets, trying to help as many Dalnorians as he could. He grabbed hover cars with giant green hands from his ring. He held them steady as the passengers climbed out. His ring placed big green cushions between crashing cars.

Hal gritted his teeth and beads of sweat formed on his forehead. The Green Lantern had to use every bit of concentration to keep the people safe. Even though he was powerful, he was still just one man. The city was full of haywire hover cars.

"Power levels at 80%," reported the ring.

"I have to find out what's causing this madness before my ring runs out of juice," he said. "Ring, analyze these hover cars. Find out what's wrong with them."

Suddenly, all of the cars stopped. They shut off and crashed to the ground.

"Nothing unusual," said the ring.

"Nothing unusual?" asked Hal. "These things go crazy, and you can't find anything wrong with them?"

Hal thought it was odd that the hover cars dropped dead just as his ring began scanning them. *Could there be someone behind all this?* he wondered. *Someone must know the power of my ring.*

"Help!" yelled a terrified voice.

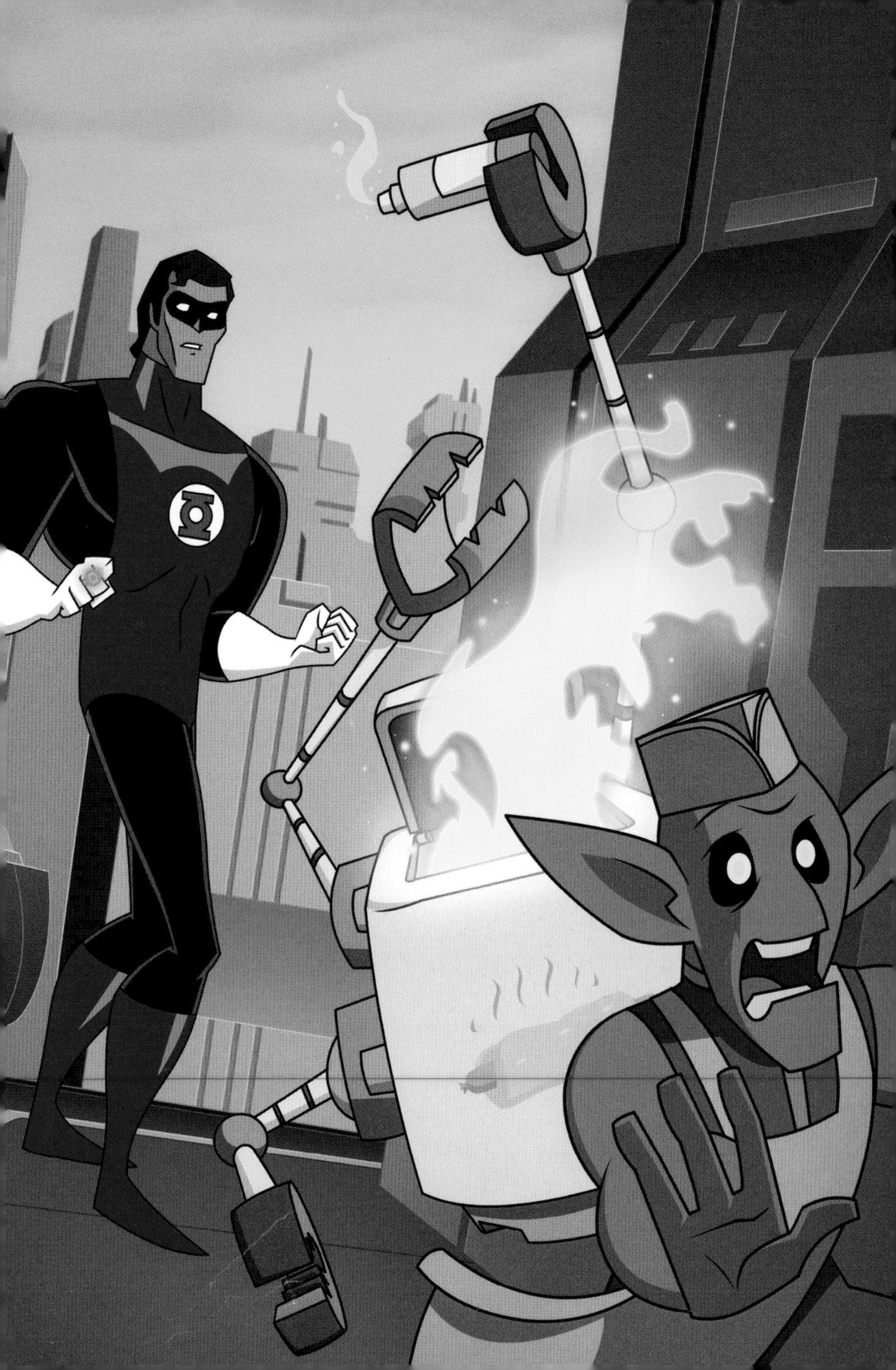

Hal flew down the street toward the cries. He turned a corner and saw a Dalnorian man running down the sidewalk. The man wore a white apron. His eyes were wide and his arms were flailing. Some kind of creature was chasing him.

Hal raised his fist. His ring glowed at the ready. Yet, as he approached, Hal saw that it wasn't a creature chasing the Dalnorian. It was a food cart. The automated cart rolled after the man. Four long robotic arms grabbed at him. Its oven door flapped open like a mouth. **WHAM! WHAM!** Flames blasted from the oven, shooting at the fleeing Dalnorian. **WHOOOOSH!**

Hal hurried toward the runaway cart. He created a giant green fire extinguisher and blasted the blaze. **SPLASH!**

The flames died out, but the arms reached up for Hal. He brought down the bottom of the fire extinguisher. The super hero smashed the cart flat.

"This is getting plain weird," Hal said.

Suddenly, a man and woman ran screaming from a nearby building. The Dalnorian version of a blender chased after them. Its base had split into four legs, and it galloped down the sidewalk. Its sharp mixing blades spun after the couple.

Hal threw a wrench in its plans — a giant monkey wrench! He smashed the blender with a construct from his ring.

Before he knew it, Dalnorians poured out of all the buildings. They were being chased by machines of all kinds. Kitchen gadgets sliced at them with sharp knives.

Entire entertainment systems sprouted legs and chased people, wielding speakers like clubs.

Hal Jordan flew over the city streets trying to help whoever he could. He created giant hammers that smashed a crazy compactor. He made a giant pair of scissors with his ring that cut the wires that were wrapped around some Dalnorians. He formed a giant green dartboard to catch flying nails from an automated nail gun.

"Power levels at 70%," his ring reported.

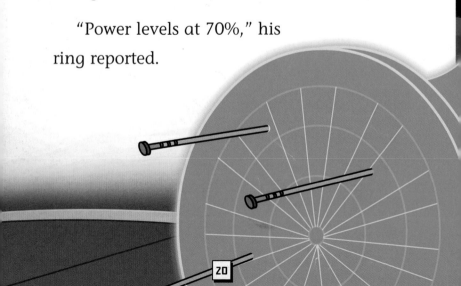

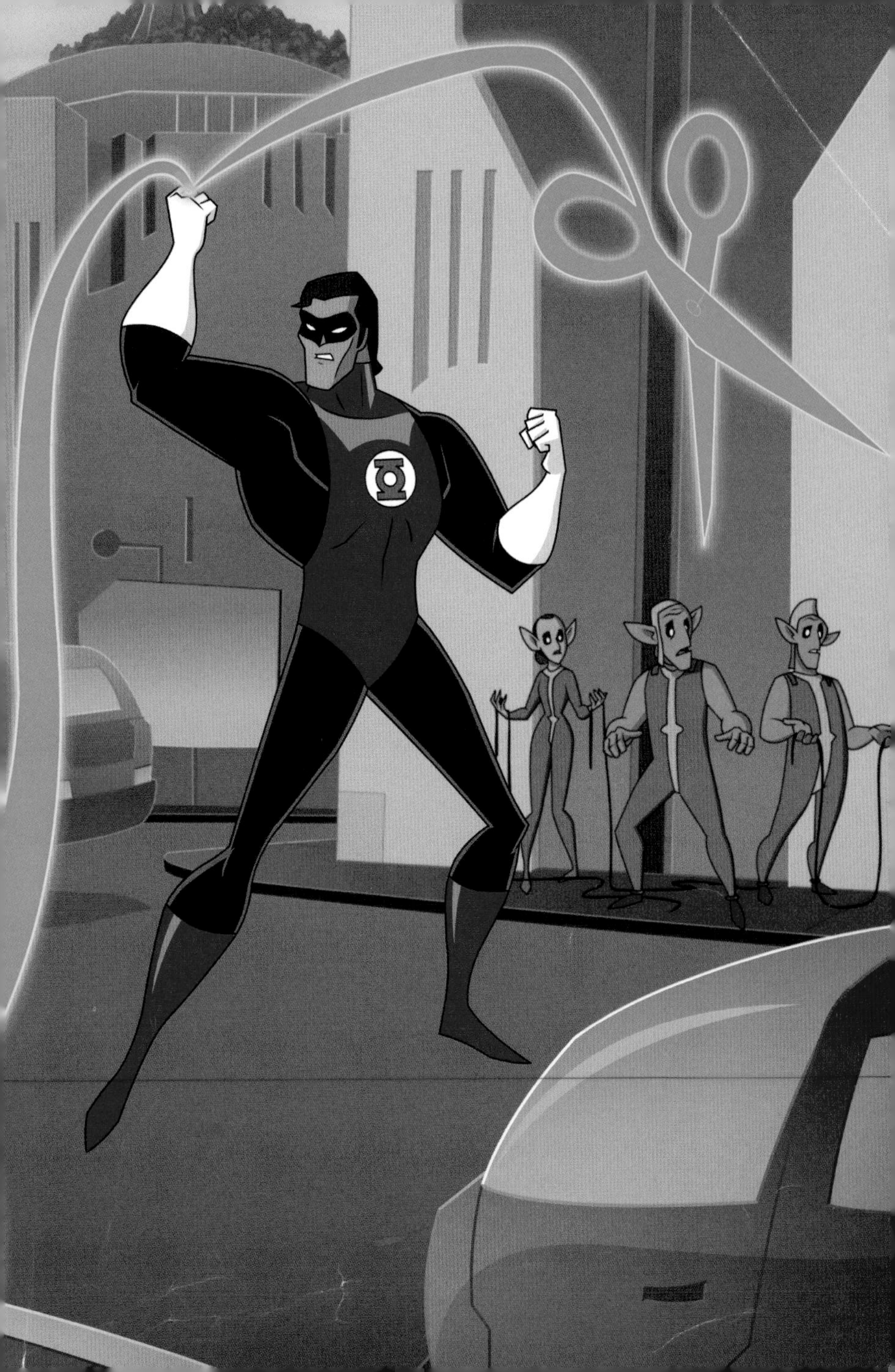

CHAPTER 3

THE TERROR OF TEKIK

"I don't have enough power left to save everyone," Hal said. "I need to stop this at the source." He held up a fist. "Ring, analyze the rampaging machines. What's causing them to attack?"

Below him, a small squad of electric fans advanced on a young couple. The gadgets' sharp blades blurred as they moved in. Hal created a giant leaf blower and aimed it at them. The machines sparked and smoked as they tumbled away.

"Analysis complete," said the ring.

"Well?" asked Hal. "Don't keep me in suspense. What's behind this techno-mayhem?"

"The machines are being controlled by an electronic signal," reported the ring.

Hal's lips tightened. "Take me to the source of that signal," he demanded.

With the ring guiding him, Hal flew high above the city. He soared into the scattered clouds. He saw nothing.

ZZRRRRTT! A yellow energy beam shot past his head. Hal turned as another attack came. **ZZRRRRTT!** He strengthened his shield just in time. It protected him, but the heavy blast sent him flying backward.

"What was that?" he asked.

"The source of the signal," said the ring.

Hal veered around a cloud and spotted his enemy. A large robot with a jet pack hovered in the sky. Its chrome body gleamed under Dalnore's two suns. The villain stared at Hal with bright yellow eyes. Its eyes weren't all that were yellow. A yellow ring glowed on its finger, and familiar black and yellow symbol adorned its chest. The robot was a member of the Sinestro Corps!

"Ah, the great Hal Jordan," the robot said with an electronic voice. "It will be a pleasure smashing you."

The robot lashed out with a yellow beam from his ring. The beam formed a giant block that hurtled toward the Green Lantern.

"Beaten by some bucket-of-bolts?" Hal said with a laugh. "I don't think so."

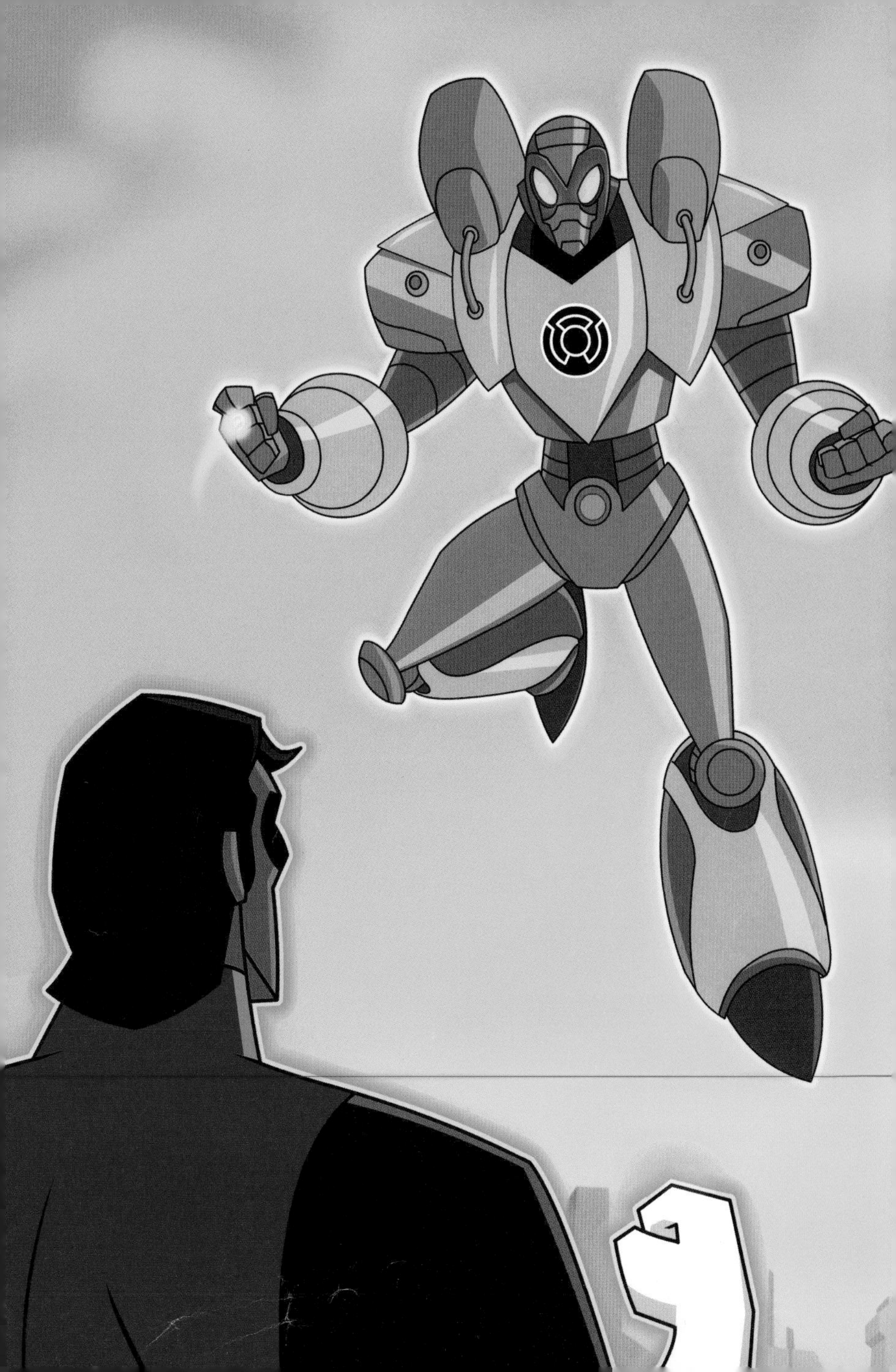

Hal had his ring create an oversized jackhammer. **CRAAAAACK!** It pierced the block and chiseled it in two. The two halves flew past Hal before vanishing.

"I assure you that I am no mere robot," boasted the Sinestro Corps member. "I am Tekik, and I will rule this planet." The evil robot lashed out with another yellow beam.

"Not going to happen," said Hal. He threw up a green shield, ready for this attack. The blast pushed him back a few feet. Then he shot back energy beams of his own. **BZZZT! BZZZT!**

Tekik dodged the sudden attack. "On my planet, robots were servants," he explained. "When my creators reprogrammed me with emotions, I felt anger. I wanted my creators to feel fear, so I uploaded a fear code into all other robots."

"They terrorized our former masters just as I'm terrorizing the people of this world!" Tekik extended a metallic arm and aimed his ring at Hal. Three large yellow spheres appeared. They flew toward the Green Lantern.

"You won't bully them for long," said Hal. His ring formed a giant tennis racket. As the spheres swooped in, he swatted them away. **THWACK!** He sent the last one flying back toward Tekik.

Hal laughed. "You're not even creative enough to come up with anything more than basic shapes," he said.

BOOM! Tekik blasted the remaining sphere with an energy beam. "You'll find that I'm *quite* creative," replied the robot.

Suddenly, Hal heard screams.

Hal left the laughing robot and raced to the city. The crazed machines and appliances were no longer simply attacking the Dalnorians. Instead, machines swarmed onto the people. They stuck fast as if each person was a walking magnet.

Hal landed in front of a woman. She was being plastered with several kinds of small machines.

"Hang on, ma'am," he said as he rushed to help. The super hero tried pulling off one of the machines, but it didn't budge.

Just then, Hal heard something behind him. He turned to see another Dalnorian completely covered in machines. The devices locked together, forming a large shell around the man. Trapped inside, the Dalnorian stared at Hal with blank eyes. The man was now a robot himself!

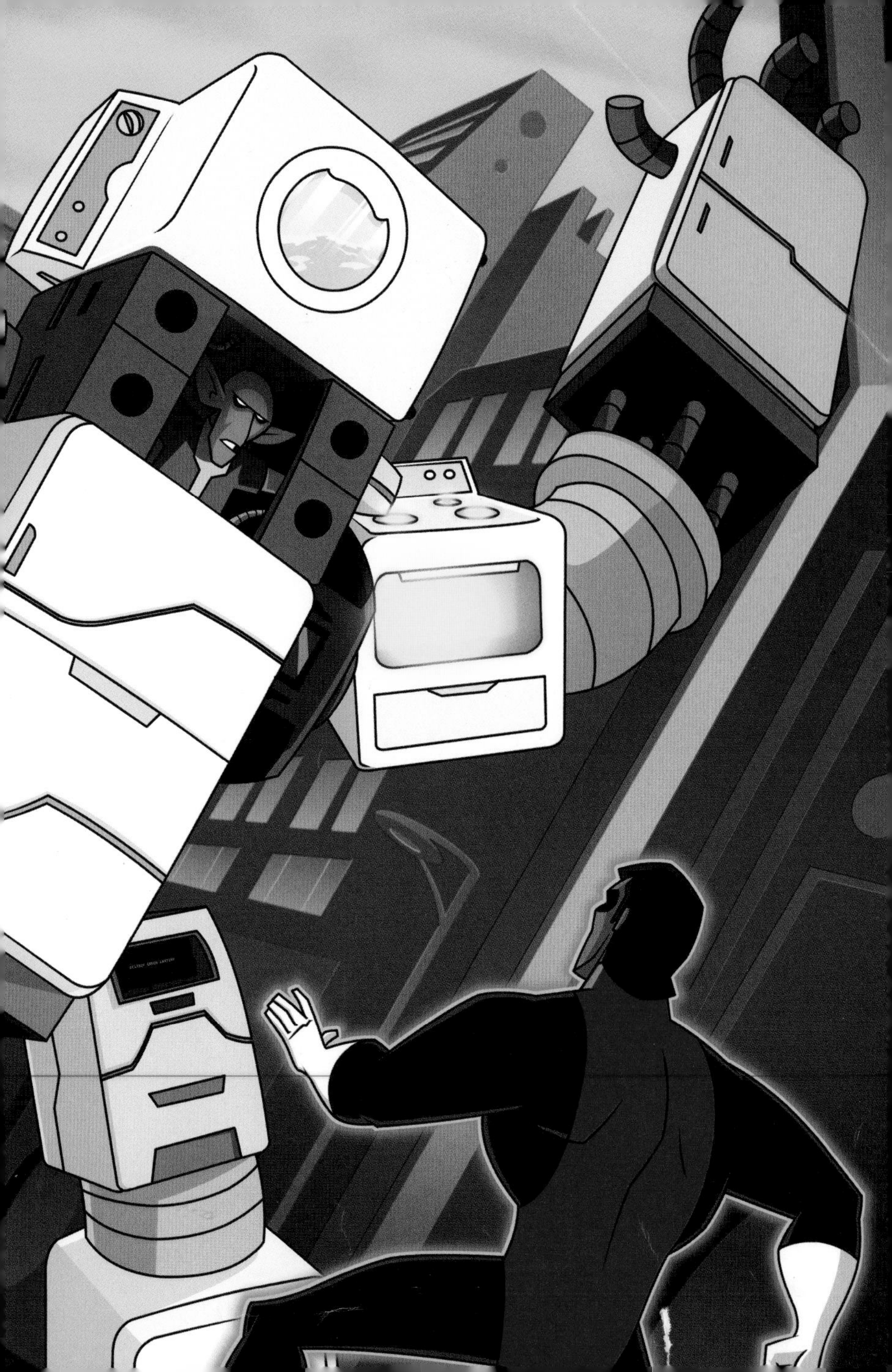

The robot backhanded him. Hal flew across the street and slammed into a building. His body made a crater in the stone wall. Hal shook his head, dazed.

As he climbed from the wall, more robots marched forward. Each robot was formed around a dazed Dalnorian. Hal staggered across the sidewalk as the metal-covered men and women moved in. Soon, the entire street was filled with robots.

Hal was surrounded.

CHAPTER 4

ROBOT RAMPAGE

Hal Jordan flew into the air as the robots lunged for him. A few smashed into each other below. The Dalnorians inside seemed unharmed. In fact, they seemed completely unaware of what their bodies were doing.

"Don't worry," he shouted down at them. "I'll stop the guy who's behind this!"

Something hit Hal from behind. As he tumbled forward he saw one of the new robots floating behind him. Flames blasted from its feet as it hovered in the air.

POW! Another hit sent him reeling. More robots rose from the ground. Hal ducked as another swung at him. He zoomed upward as two more tried to tackle him in midair.

Hundreds of robots filled the sky above the city. Hal couldn't dodge them forever. He had to stop the source.

Hal created a sonic boom as he rocketed away. **THWOOOOMMMMMM!!**

He found Tekik floating over the fields outside the city. "My army is growing," the robot announced. "After all the Dalnorians are upgraded, I'll move on to another planet." He blasted yellow beams of energy at the Green Lantern. "Maybe Earth."

Hal dodged the beams as he zeroed in on his foe. "Not on my watch!" Large green boxing gloves formed on Hal's fists.

Before the robot could attack again, Hal landed the first punch. **WHAM!** Tekik crashed to the ground. His metal body plowed a long trench across a field before he came to a stop.

Hal landed in front of him. "Last chance, Tekik," he shouted. His ring glowed as he moved toward the downed robot.

Tekik looked up and laughed. A Dalnorian robot landed between Hal and Tekik. They landed all around him. More and more were diving from the sky. Hal formed a green dome as they flew at him.

Soon, his protective shield was covered with robots. Hal closed his eyes and concentrated. He would need all the willpower he could muster. **BOOM!**

The mass of robots exploded outward!

Hal flew into the air and extended his right arm. He made his ring create spheres around each of the flying robots. He steadied his trembling wrist with his other hand. Thousands of robots were now trapped inside their own shields.

Hal narrowed his eyes at Tekik. "You wanted an army? Well, here they come!" he shouted. Green Lantern sent the balls flying toward the Sinestro Corp member. Hal knew that the shields would protect the Dalnorians inside. He just hoped they would damage Tekik at the same time.

"No!" yelled Tekik.

The robot dodged the first few spheres. Then, as they hit him, the robot was tossed around like a metal rag doll. He fell to the ground as the green balls piled atop him.

Soon, all the robots went limp. They floated inside their spheres, unconscious. Hal released them from the shields, and they remained piled atop Tekik. The Green Lantern landed and looked up at the enormous mound of metal.

"Now, I just need to find a way to release these people from the machines," he said.

RUMMMMMMMMBLE! The ground trembled under his feet. Hal almost lost his balance. He rose into the air, away from the unsteady soil. The pile of robots began to move! The metallic bodies churned as the mound grew taller and taller.

As the mass of metal rose toward the sky, it began taking shape — it formed a head, then shoulders, and then arms. All of the Dalnorian robots fused together to create a colossal version of Tekik!

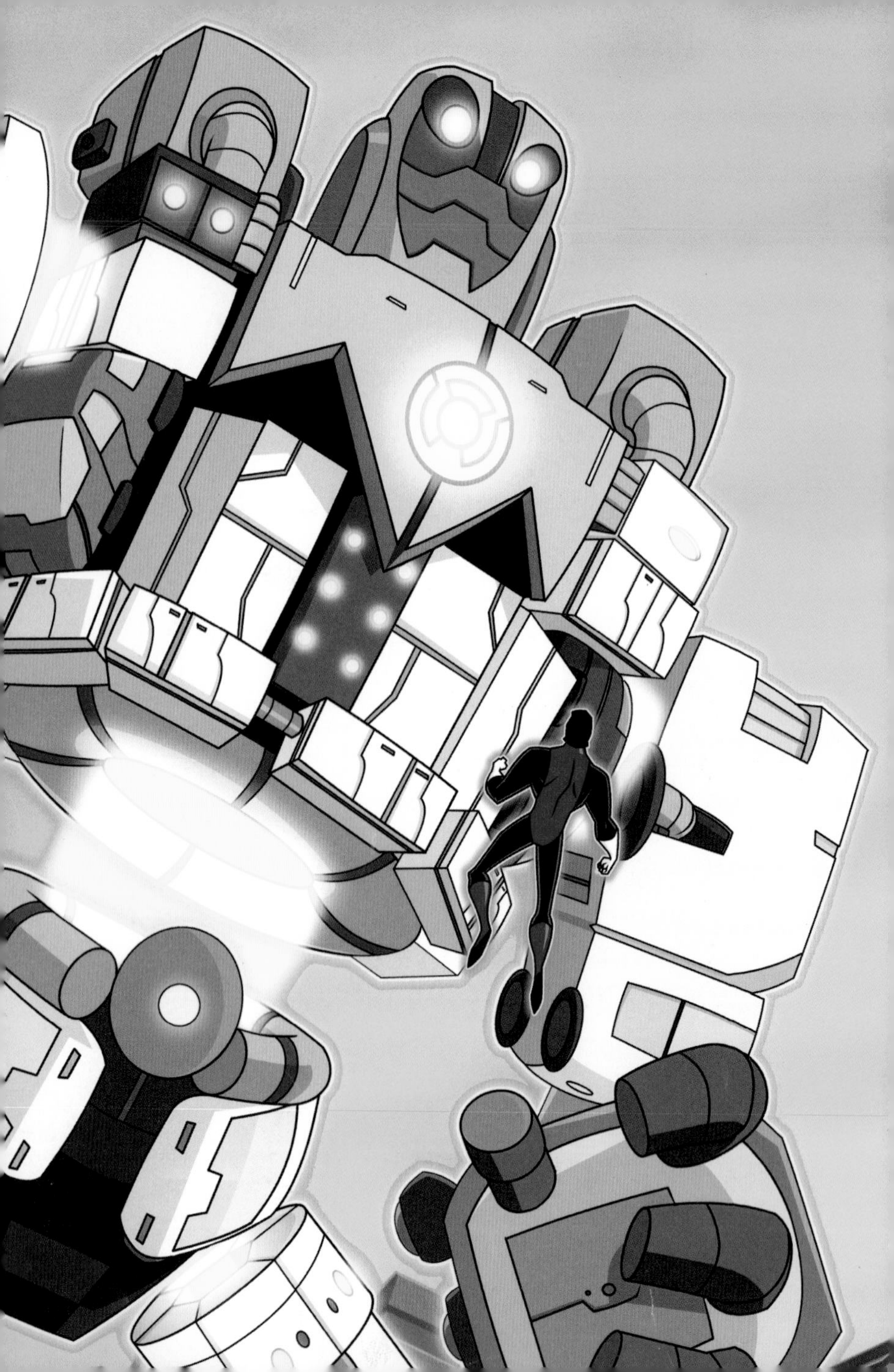

When the robot was fully formed, it stood over twenty stories tall. Its large yellow eyes glowed brighter than the planet's two suns.

"Puny human," bellowed the giant robot. "I have a 42-Zettabyte drive for a brain. You can never outsmart me!"

"Well, if I can't match your brains," Hal said, "at least I can match your strength."

His ring glowed as he concentrated. Bright green light formed all around him. It took the shape of a giant robot. Now Hal had his own oversized fighting machine!

The enormous Tekik swung at Hal's robot suit. Hal blocked the punch and landed one of his own. **KA-BOOM!** The hit echoed for miles. The giant evil robot flew backward, landing on its back.

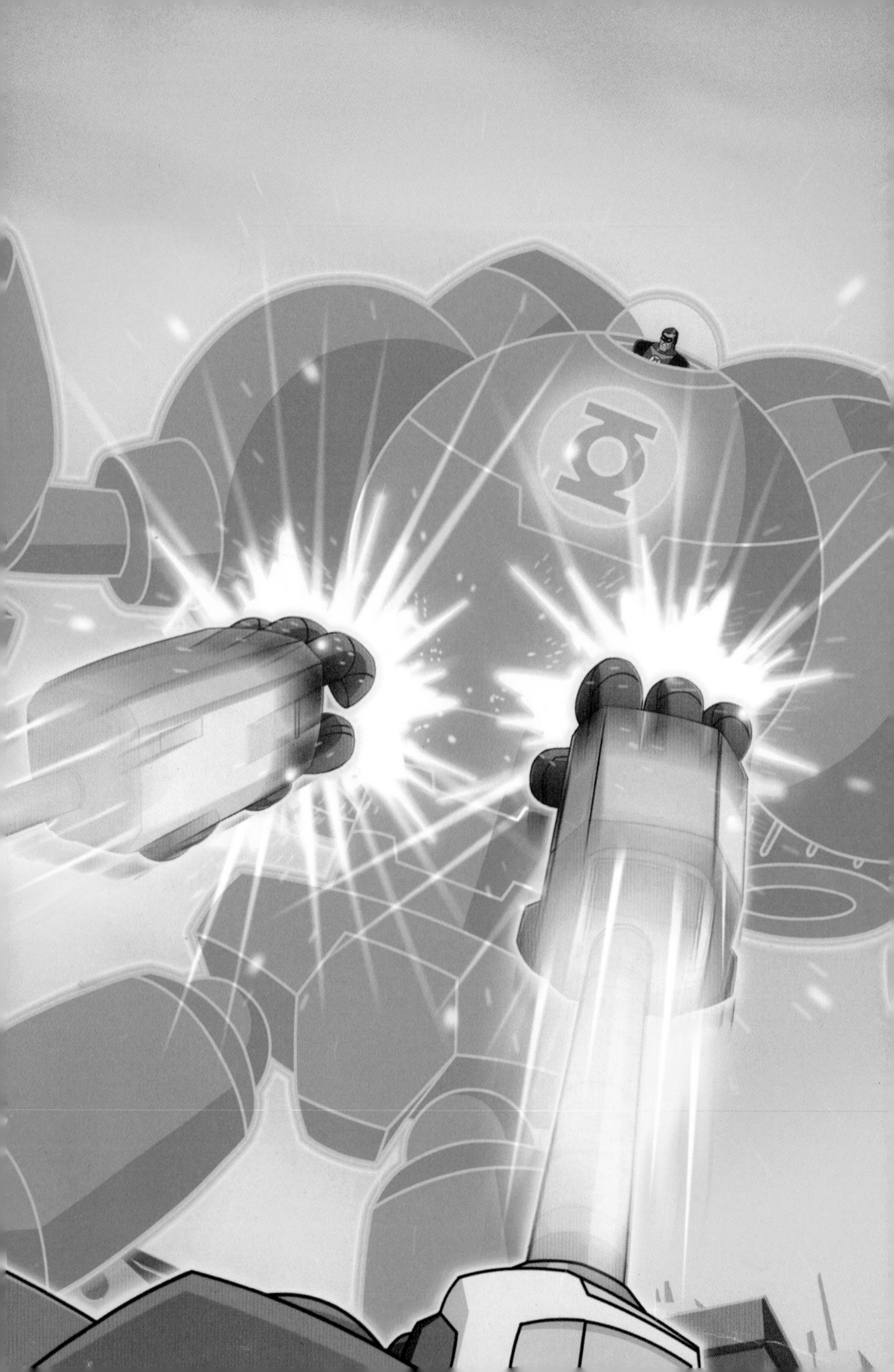

As Hal moved his robot closer, the giant Tekik raised its arms. Both fists shot from their wrists. They flew across the field and struck Hal's robot in the chest. He and his robot flew backward, plowing into the soil.

"Power levels at 40%," his ring reported.

"Yeah, yeah," Hal said as he got his robot to its feet.

Still connected by long cables, Tekik's fists retracted back to their arms. The evil robot stood and charged. Hal's robot was barely on its feet when Tekik tackled it. Once on top, Tekik began pounding him.

"Power levels at 20%," said his ring. "19% . . . 18% . . ."

With all his willpower, Hal shoved Tekik away. The robot flew back and landed on its feet. Its fists were raised, ready to attack.

Hal didn't have enough power to maintain his green robot suit. Soon, his ring would be drained, and he would be powerless. "Too bad I can't give all his Zettabytes a computer virus," Hal said.

Hal got rid of his big green robot. Then he floated to the ground and landed gently among the trampled crops.

The Tekik robot ran up to him. "I will squash you like the bug you are!" The robot raised a giant foot and a shadow fell over the Green Lantern.

Tekik slammed his massive foot onto Hal Jordan. The robot boomed with metallic laughter.

THE HEART OF THE PROBLEM

But when the colossal Tekik robot lifted its foot, Hal Jordan wasn't there! Only a huge footprint remained in the ground.

Hal couldn't give Tekik a computer virus. He could, however, *act* like a virus and travel inside the robot's body. He had flown up a narrow passage inside the robot's ankle.

As Hal made his way up the leg, he passed the many smaller robots that formed the giant one. The Dalnorians were still dazed inside their metallic shells.

Hal had to find Tekik fast. He didn't know how long those people could last trapped inside all that machinery.

"Where are you, Jordan?" asked Tekik. Hal could feel the giant robot moving around, looking for him. "Where are you hiding, Green Lantern?"

"I'm closer than you think," Hal muttered as he flew through the robot's waist.

"I heard that!" shouted Tekik. "Very clever, Earthman!"

Hal spotted Tekik as soon as he flew into the robot's chest. The Sinestro Corps member was embedded inside a tangled mass of wires and machinery. He was at the heart of the giant robot. In fact, Tekik *was* the robot's heart.

"This is going to be easier than I thought," said Hal.

Something caught his ankle. Hal glanced back to see one of the Dalnorian robots gripping his leg. Another one grabbed his other leg. A robot above him snagged his left arm.

Tekik laughed. "Not quite," he shouted.

Hal fought his way free from their metallic grasp. He pushed closer to Tekik only to be slowed by more robots. The entire place was made of robots and there were grabbing hands everywhere. They all worked together to keep him from getting closer to Tekik.

Hal pushed through the clutching hands as far as he could. He was only a few feet from Tekik, but he could move no closer.

In fact, he couldn't move at all. Hal Jordan was trapped.

"Perhaps I should make a robot out of you," said Tekik. "Having a Green Lantern in my army will make me even more powerful."

"I already have a job," Hal sneered. He continued struggling.

"Maybe I'll make you trade places with me," Tekik suggested. "You could be the heart of this powerful robot."

That gave Hal an idea. He aimed his ring at Tekik and produced a green defibrillator. The medical device was a small box with two paddles on long spiraling cords that doctors use to shock a patient's heart. Hal decided to use it on the heart of this giant robot — Tekik!

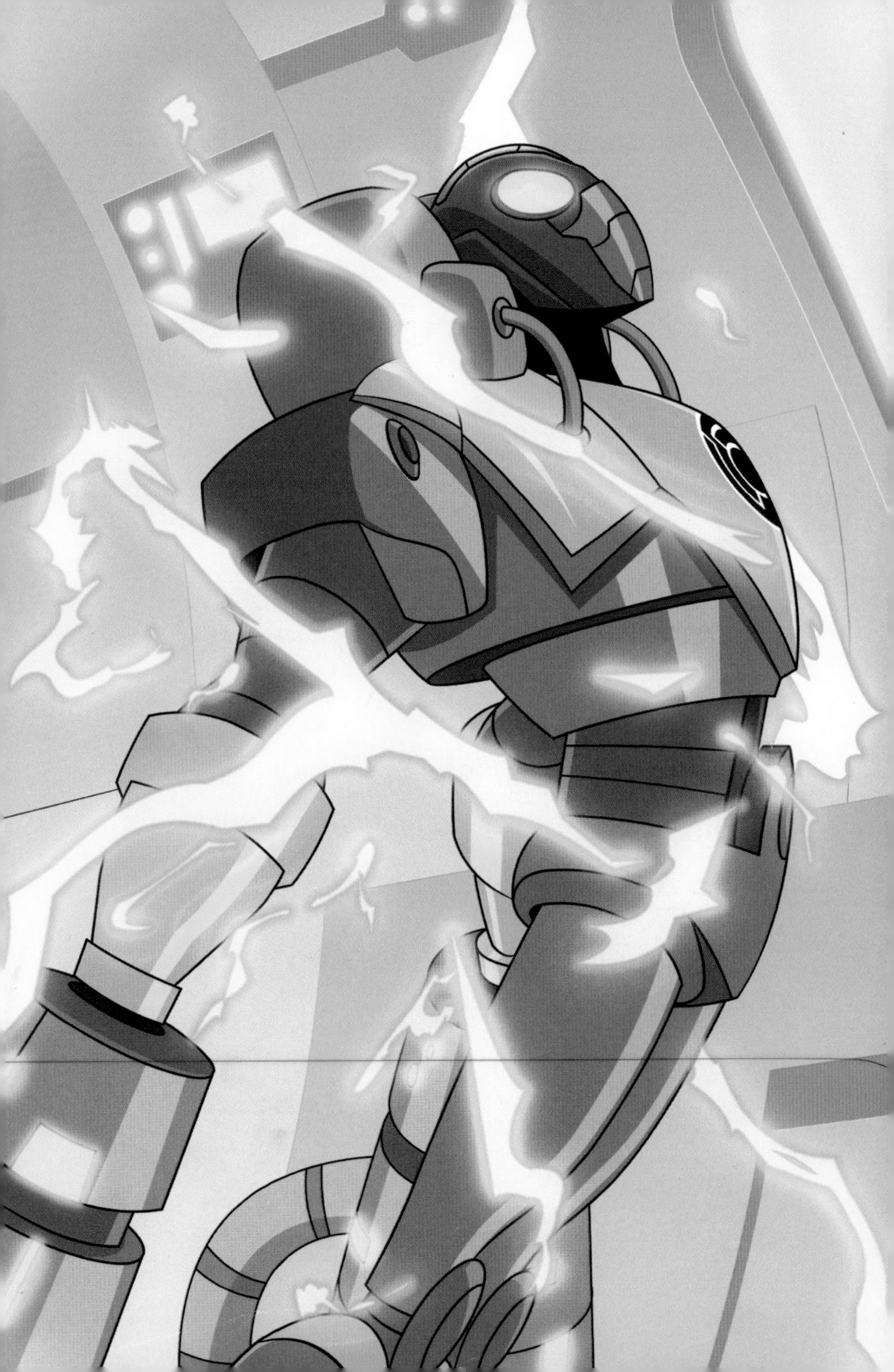

"What are you doing?!" yelled Tekik.

The paddles moved toward him. Their long cords pulled tight as they stuck to Sinestro Corp member's chest. "It's time to reboot your hard drive," said Hal.

"No!" shouted Tekik.

ZZRRRRTT! Several thousand volts shot through Tekik's body. The robot trembled then fell unconscious. His yellow eyes slowly faded to black.

The surrounding robots released Hal as the entire structure trembled. Small robots broke free as the giant robot fell apart.

Thinking fast, Hal had his ring attach thousands of green parachutes to the falling Dalnorians. As they floated to the ground, all of the devices, gadgets, and machinery fell away from their bodies.

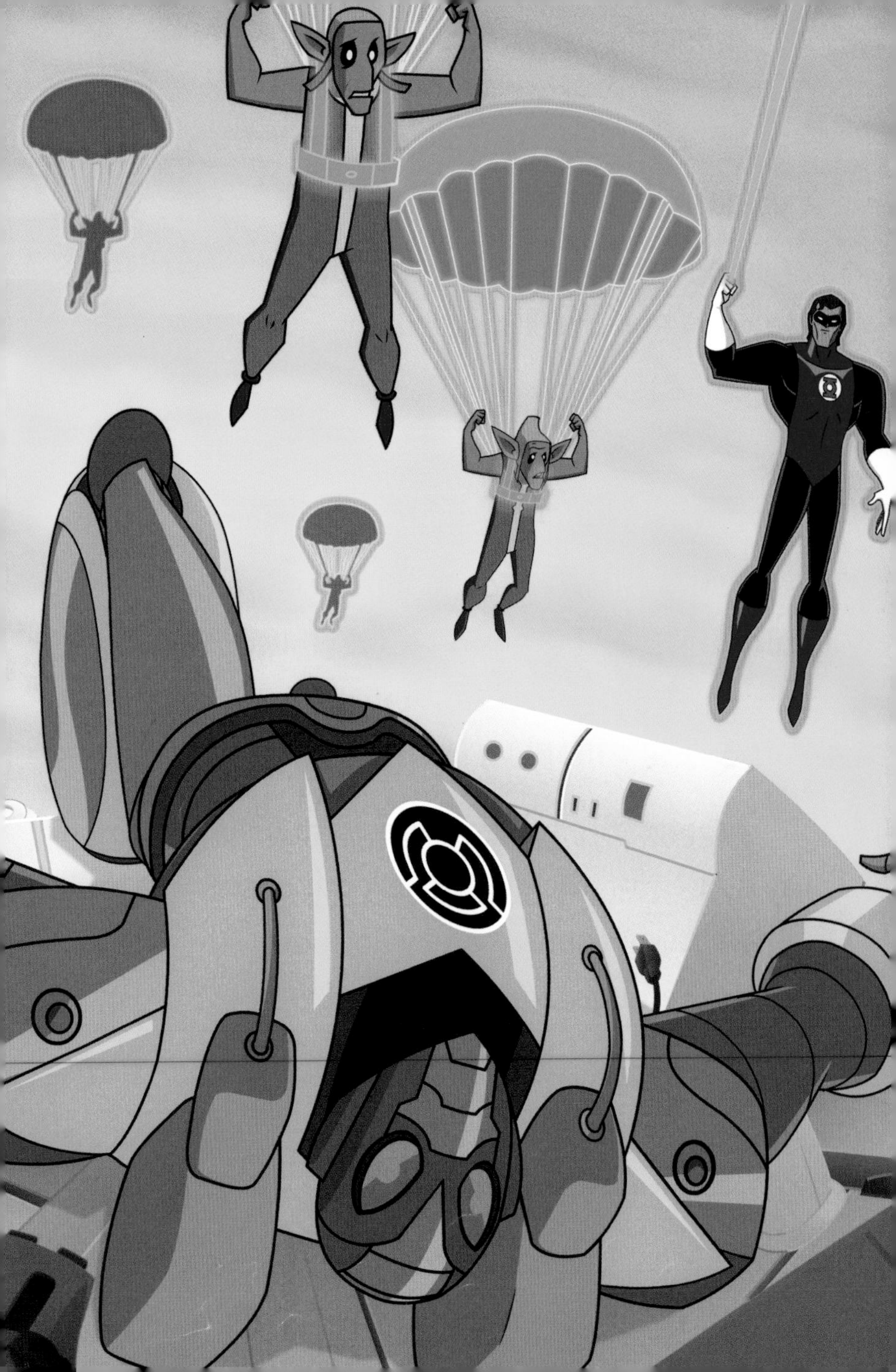

Soon, thousands of dazed Dalnorians stood among piles of junked machines.

Hal drifted to the ground. He held the unconscious Tekik inside a large green sphere.

"What happened?" asked a man. "I hardly remember a thing!"

"This evil robot took control of your machines and then you," Hal replied. "But don't worry. The Green Lantern Corps has a prison cell with his name on it."

Keeping the sphere tethered to his ring, Hal rose into the air. He flew out of the planet's atmosphere and into space. He headed straight for the planet Oa.

Once he reached Oa, he would lock Tekik away in the Green Lantern prison — the Sciencells.

"After I drop off the prisoner and recharge my ring, I think I'll take some time off," Hal said to himself. He didn't feel like climbing into another fighter jet just yet. For now, he'd had quite enough of "being one with a machine."

TEKIK

BIRTHPLACE: Potter-59-3

OCCUPATION: Sinestro Corps

HEIGHT: 7' 1"   **WEIGHT:** 475lbs.

EYES: Yellow   **HAIR:** None

POWERS/ABILITIES: capable of human emotions; able to download a "fear code" into any robot or machine; high-tech weaponry; flight; impenetrable armor.

BIOGRAPHY

Manufactured on the distant planet Potter-59-3, Tekik was an obedient robot. But unlike other robotic units, Tekik's master gave his mechanical servant emotions. Soon, Tekik grew angry at his master's constant demands. Seeking revenge, the angered android uploaded a "fear code" into every robot on his home planet. Nothing on the planet survived — except Tekik. He left the lost world shortly after and became a member of the Sinestro Corps, hoping to spread his fear throughout the universe.

2814

The Guardians of the Universe divided space into 3,600 sections called sectors. Tekik's home planet, Potter-59-3, is located in Sector 3281.

After Tekik uploaded his "fear code" into the robots on Potter-59-3, the planet never recovered. Today, it is known as the "Lost World."

Soon after leaving his home planet, Tekik joined the Sinestro Corps. This group of evildoers wears yellow power rings and hope to spread fear throughout the universe.

Tekik and other Sinestro Corps members are led by Thaal Sinestro. This evil leader was once a powerful member of the Green Lantern Corps and a mentor to Hal Jordan. However, he eventually turned against those who first gave him power.

BIOGRAPHIES

Michael A. Steele has been in the entertainment industry for almost twenty years. He worked in many capacities of film and television production from props and special effects all the way up to writing and directing. For the past fifteen years, Mr. Steele has written exclusively for family entertainment. For television and video, he wrote for shows including *WISHBONE*, *Barney & Friends,* and *Boz, The Green Bear Next Door*. He has authored over sixty books for various characters including Batman, Shrek, Spider-Man, Garfield, G.I. Joe, Speed Racer, Sly Cooper, and The Penguins of Madagascar.

Dan Schoening was born in Victoria, B.C., Canada. From an early age, Dan has had a passion for animation and comic books. Currently, Dan does freelance work in the animation and game industry and spends a lot of time with his lovely little daughter, Paige.

GLOSSARY

analyze (AN-uh-lize)—to examine something carefully in order to understand it

asteroid (ASS-tuh-roid)—a very small planet that travels around the sun

atmosphere (AT-muhss-fihr)—the mixture of gases that surrounds a planet

construct (KON-struhkt)—something built or made by the power of the mind

corps (KOR)—a group of people acting together

galaxy (GAL-uhk-see)—a very large group of stars and planets

haywire (HAY-wire)—acting wild or out of control

Mach (MAHK)—a unit for measuring an aircraft's speed; Mach 1 is the speed of sound.

transformed (transs-FORMD)—made a great change in something

virus (VYE-russ)—hidden instructions within a computer program designed to damage data

willpower (WIL-pou-ur)—the ability to control what you will and will not do

DISCUSSION QUESTIONS

1. Tekik's former master treated him poorly, so he took his anger out on others. Do you think this behavior is okay? Explain.

2. Why didn't Hal Jordan want to harm the Dalnorians inside the giant robot? Explain.

3. If you could travel to any planet in the solar system, where would you go? Why?

WRITING PROMPTS

1. Write about your own robot made of household machines. What would you use to make your mechanical soldier? Would it have toasters for feet? How about a TV for a head? Give your high-tech terror a name and draw a picture of it.

2. Write another Green Lantern adventure! Where will Hal and the Corps go next? What villain will they take on?

3. Members of the Green Lantern Corps come from all different planets. Create your own Green Lantern. What is its name? What planet does it come from? What does it look like?

MORE NEW GREEN LANTERN ADVENTURES!

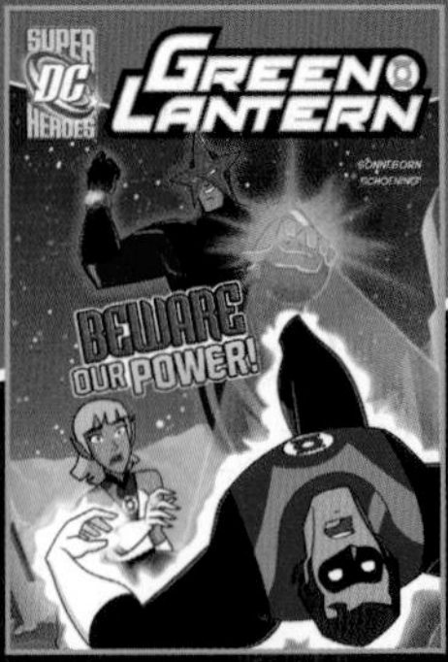

SUPER DC HEROES
GREEN LANTERN
BEWARE OUR POWER!

BEWARE OUR POWER!

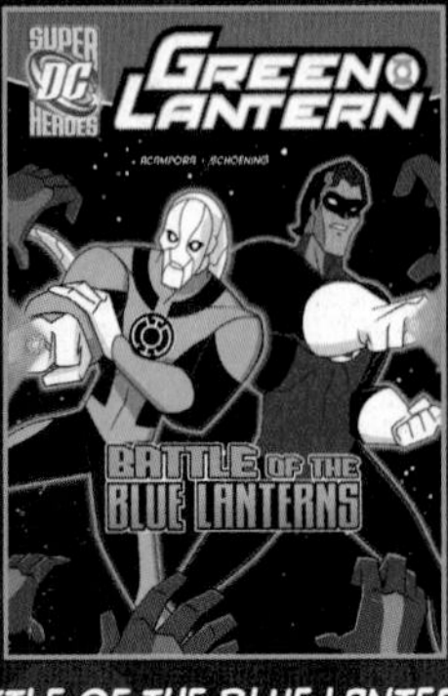

SUPER DC HEROES
GREEN LANTERN
BATTLE OF THE BLUE LANTERNS

BATTLE OF THE BLUE LANTERNS

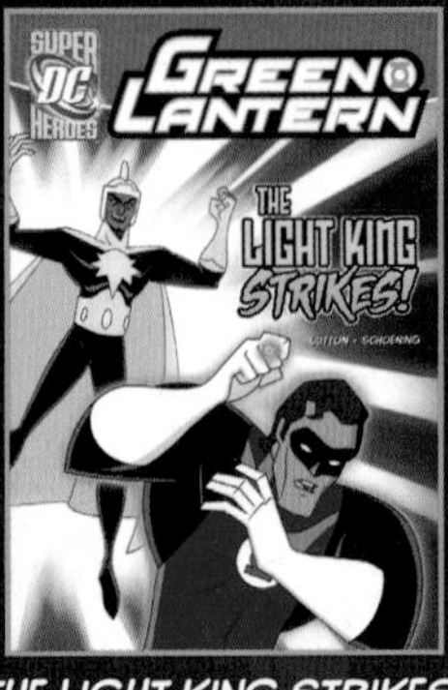

SUPER DC HEROES
GREEN LANTERN
THE LIGHT KING STRIKES!

THE LIGHT KING STRIKES!

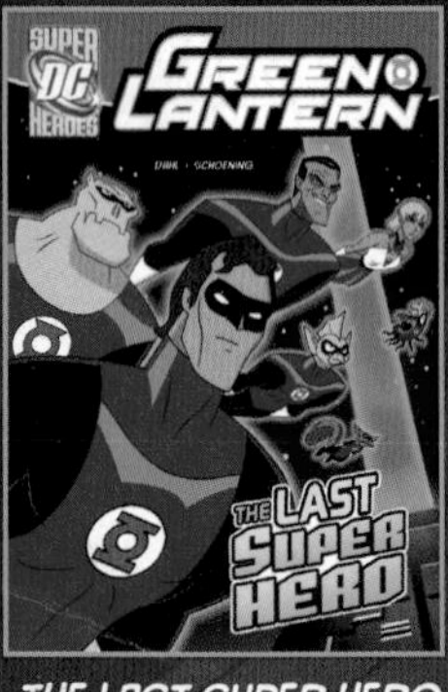

SUPER DC HEROES
GREEN LANTERN
THE LAST SUPER HERO

THE LAST SUPER HERO

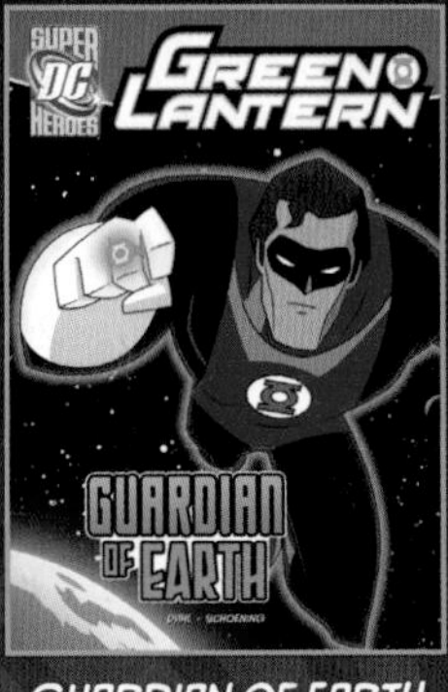

SUPER DC HEROES
GREEN LANTERN
GUARDIAN OF EARTH

GUARDIAN OF EARTH

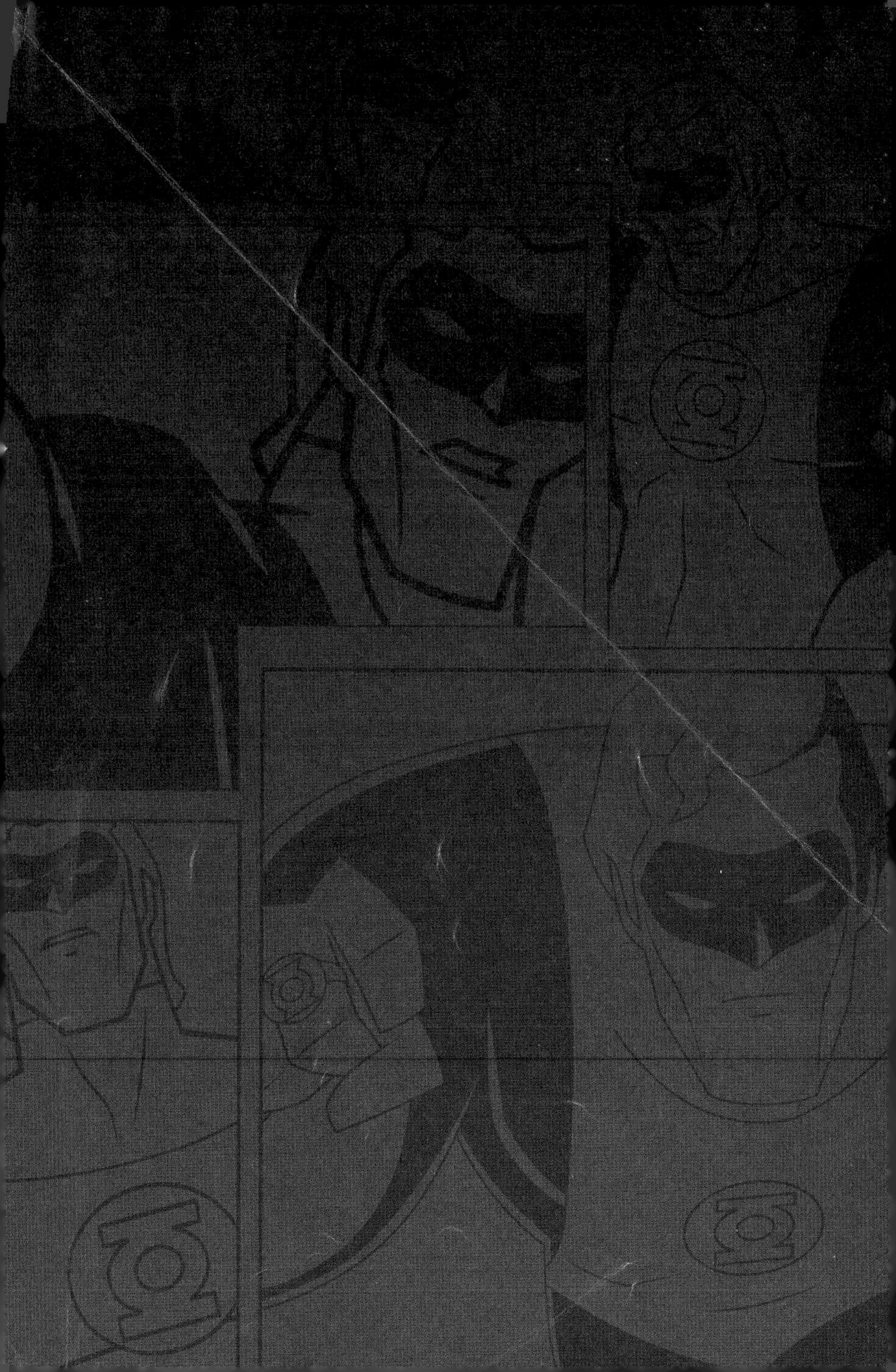

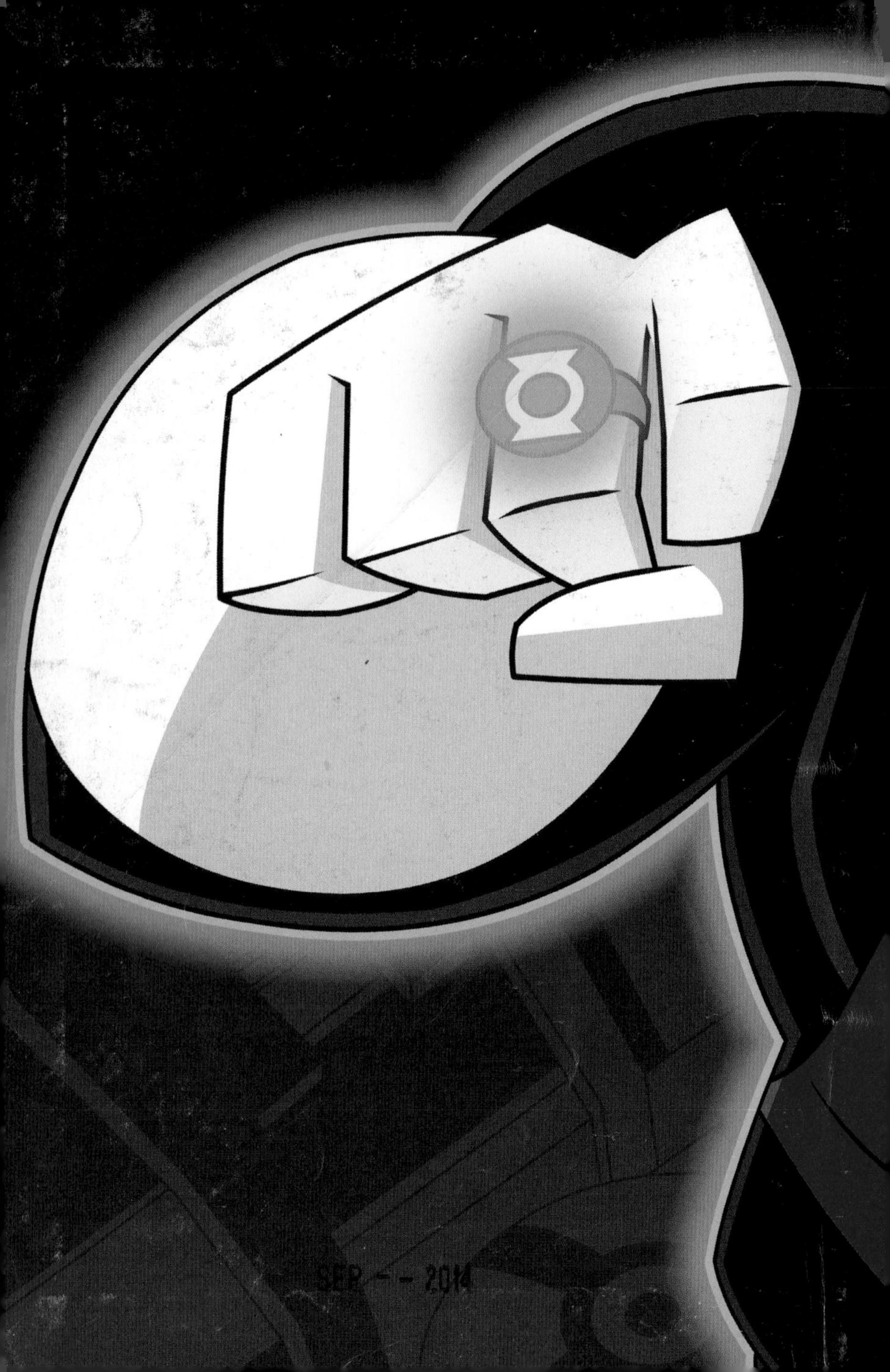